What Feels Cold?

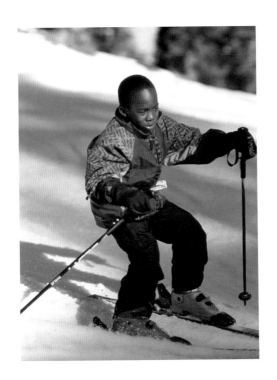

written by Pam Holden

1

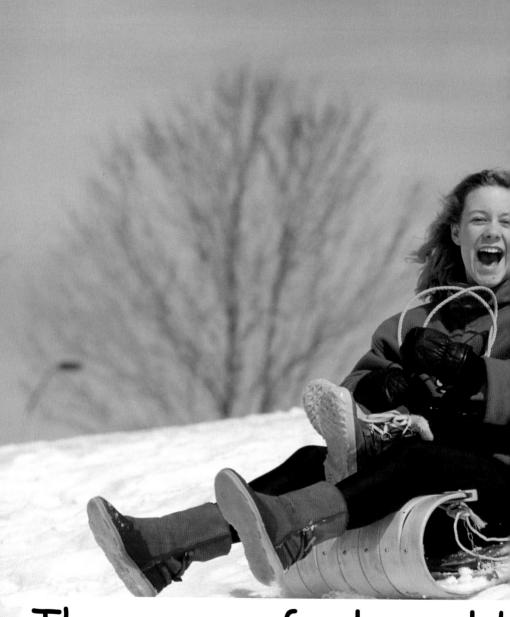

The snow feels cold

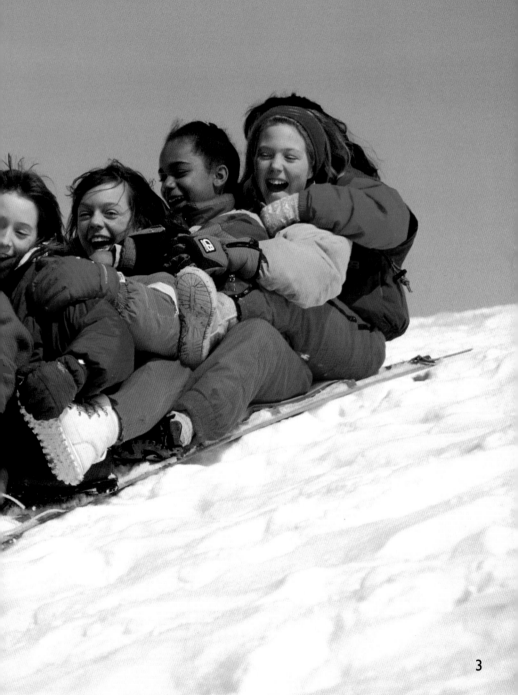

The wind feels cold.

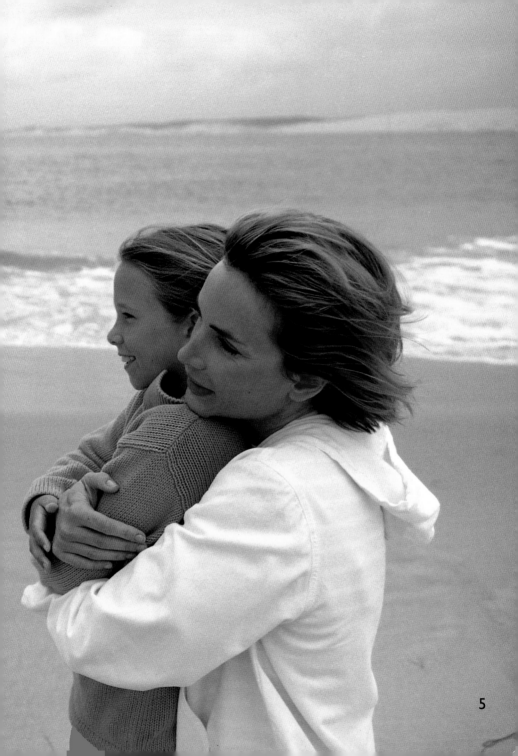

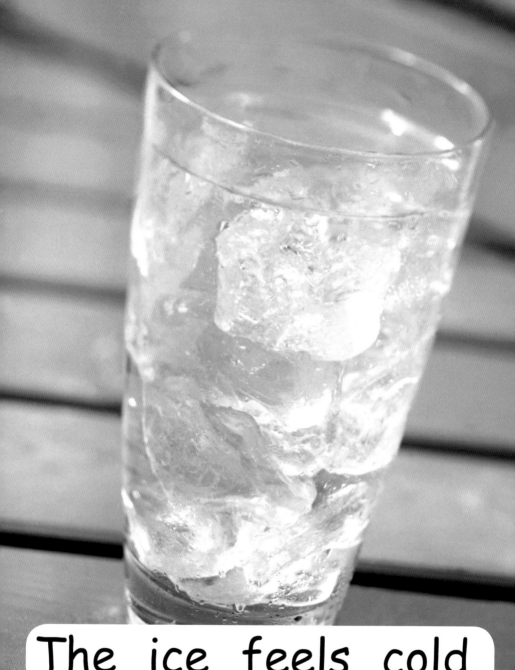

The ice feels cold.

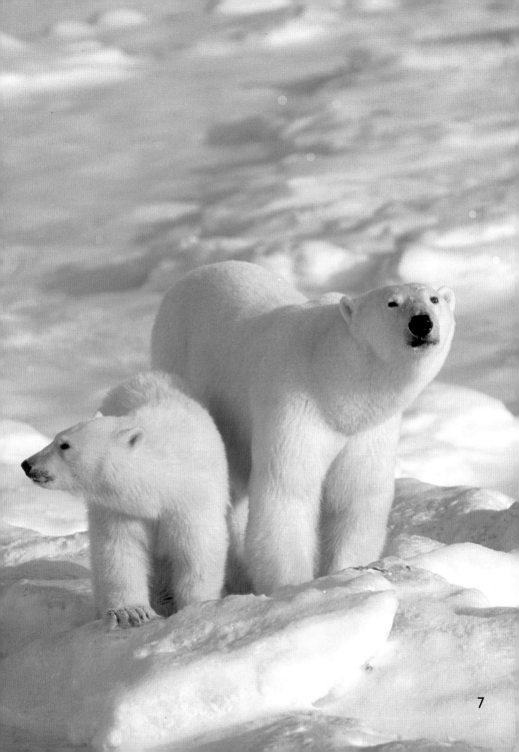

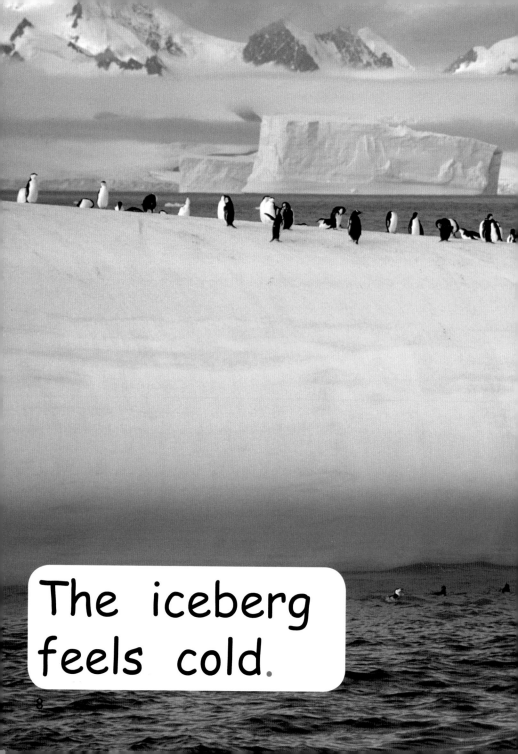

The iceberg
feels cold.

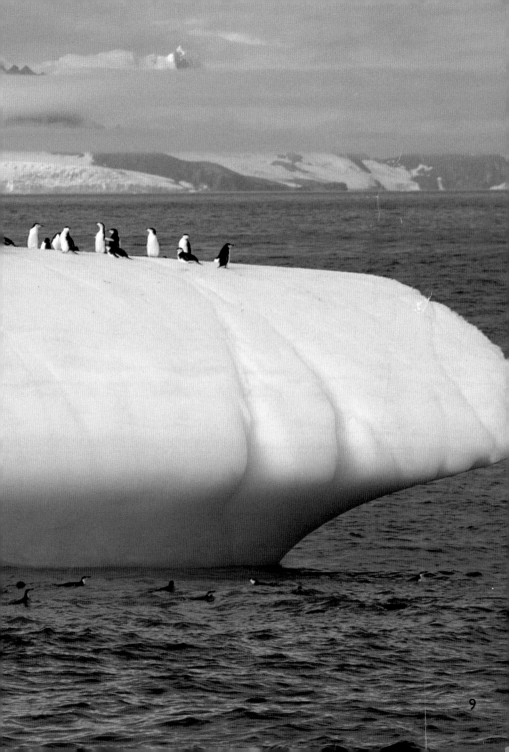

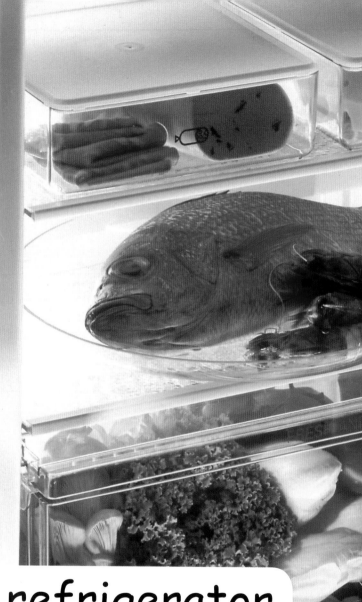

The refrigerator
feels cold.

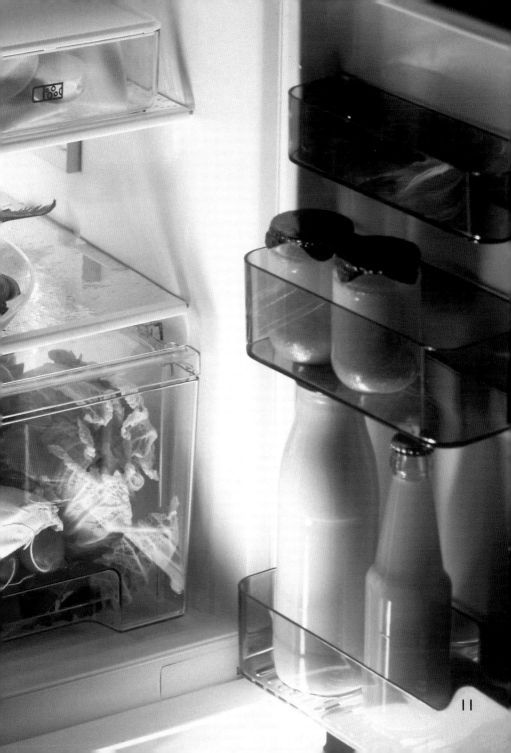

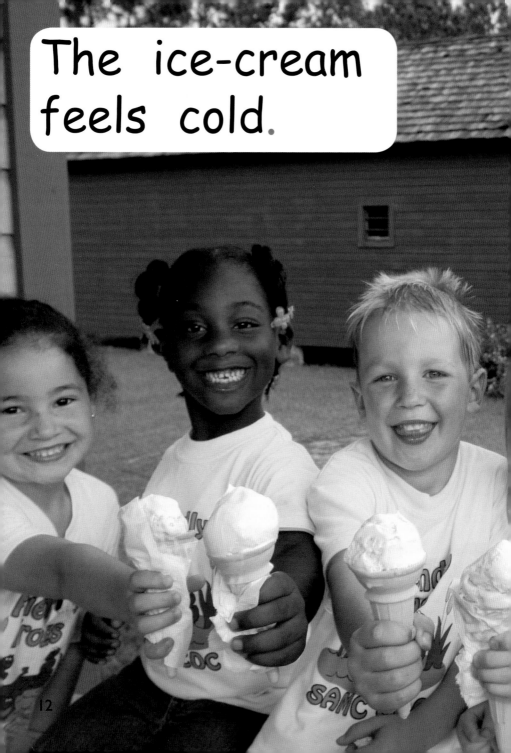

The ice-cream feels cold.

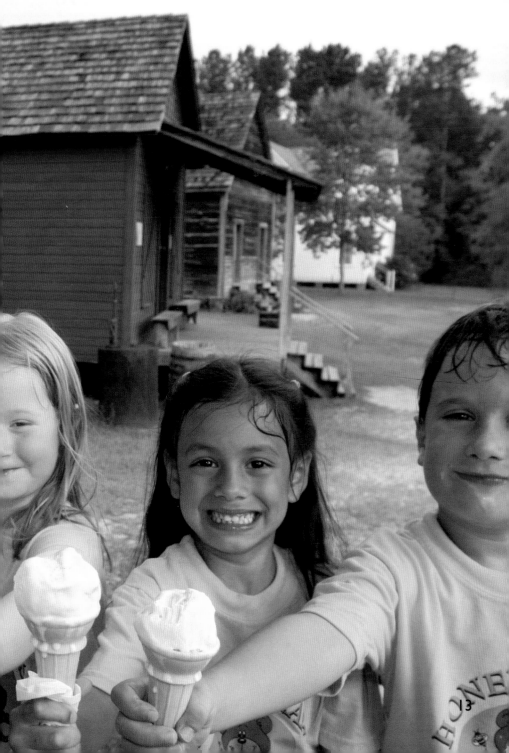

13

The snowman
feels cold.

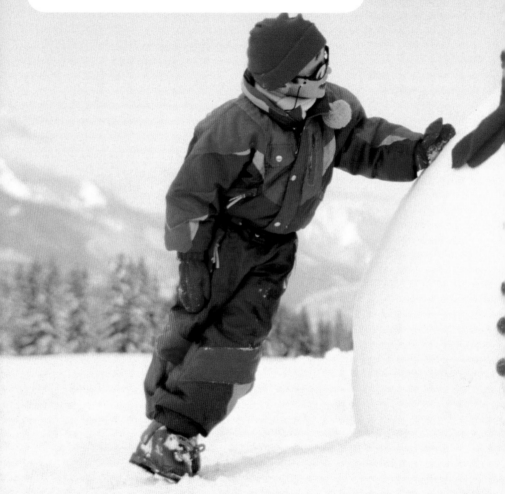

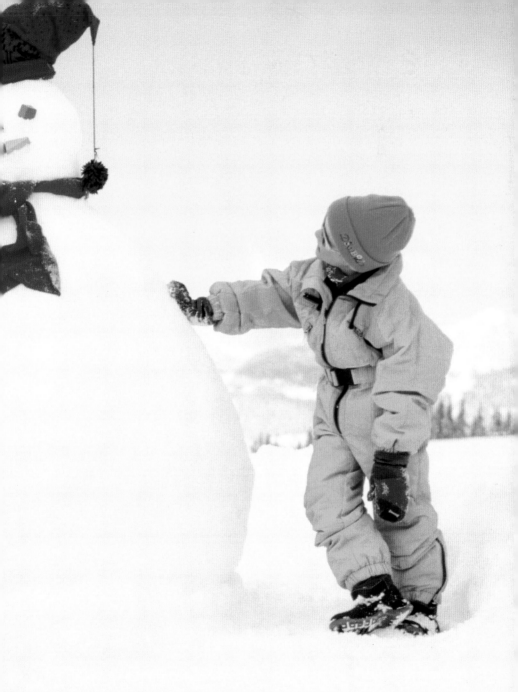

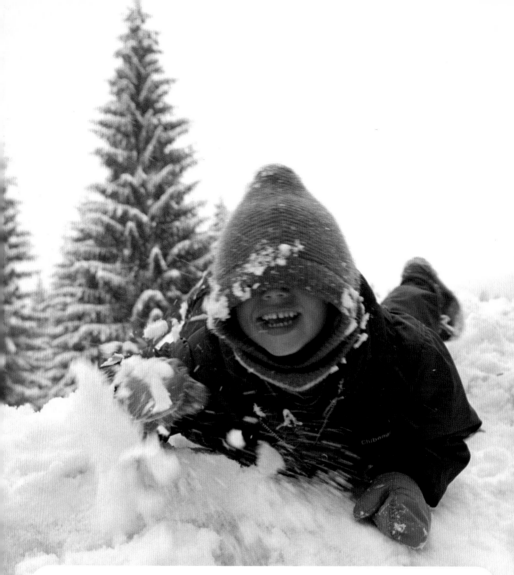

The snowball feels
very cold!